MICHA...

Pad...

DOES IT HIMSELF

Illustrated by Barry Wilkinson

COLLINS COLOUR CUBS

One day, the Browns had to go out early in order to do some shopping, so Paddington decided to have his breakfast in bed.

Paddington liked having breakfast in bed. It gave him a chance to catch up on his reading, and as a special treat Mrs. Brown left him a pile of books and magazines.

Some of them were very interesting indeed, and one in particular made him sit up and take notice.

It was called "DO-IT-YOURSELF" and it showed how to make a magazine rack.

Although the article didn't say anything about "bears" doing it themselves,
it made it all sound very simple.

In fact, it was so interesting, Paddington
dipped his paw in the hot cocoa by
mistake instead of the marmalade jar.

All of which helped him make up his mind. He would have a go himself.

Paddington wasn't the sort of bear who believed in wasting time, and he decided it wasn't worth having a proper wash if he was going to get dirty again. So, apart from cleaning his teeth, he simply passed the face flannel over his whiskers a couple of times.

Only a few days before, he'd accidentally bought a set of carpentry tools at an auction sale, and since then they had been standing idle in Mr. Brown's shed.

Now seemed a very good time to test them out.

Paddington investigated the contents of the tool box. There was a hammer, a saw, three chisels, a plane and several other things which he didn't recognise. Altogether it seemed very good value and he felt sure he would be able to make the Browns a very nice magazine rack indeed.

A few moments later, armed with a piece of plywood Mr. Brown had promised he could use, Paddington staggered outside.

Almost at once he wished he hadn't,
for there was a strong wind blowing
and he was so laden it wasn't at all
easy.

. . . which was how he came to bump
into the Browns' neighbour, Mr. Curry.

"Bear!" bellowed Mr. Curry. "What are you doing, bear?"

"Do it yourself, Mr. Curry!" exclaimed Paddington.

"Don't be impertinent, bear!" roared Mr. Curry.

"Oh, no, Mr. Curry," replied Paddington hastily. "I didn't mean you were to do it *your*self. I meant I'm going to do it *my*self. I'm making a magazine rack. Look. . . ."

. . . And he held up the book for Mr. Curry to see.

"Mm." Mr. Curry calmed down slightly. "A magazine rack, eh?" he said thoughtfully. "I'd like one of those, bear.

"As it happens," he went on, "I'm going out, so you can use my kitchen table to work on. If you make me one by the time I get back I *may* not report you for banging my nose just now."

"Thank you very much, Mr. Curry," said Paddington gloomily.

He wasn't too keen on doing jobs for the Browns' neighbour. Somehow or other they always seemed to go wrong.

Before he went out, Mr. Curry gave Paddington a long list of "don'ts" — mostly to do with not making a mess . . .

. . . but as Paddington set to work he quickly forgot them in his excitement.

Paddington had never sawn anything in two before and he found it wasn't as easy as it looked.

In fact, it got harder and harder.

He tried starting from the other side, but that was just as bad.

It wasn't until he sat down for a much needed rest that he discovered why.

There was a splintering noise and the table suddenly parted in the middle.

Paddington tried hard to think of a reason why Mr. Curry might like two small tables with only two legs each instead of one large table with four legs.

He peered hopefully at his instructions, but there was nothing in them about mending next-door neighbours' tables which had been accidentally sawn in half.

Paddington wasn't the sort of bear to be beaten, so after carefully spreading some glue along the edge of the two halves he tried propping them up on some cardboard boxes . . .

. . . nailing them both together for good measure.

To finish things off, he rubbed some marmalade along the join in the hope that it would disguise the crack.

But even with the curtains drawn he had to admit that Mr. Curry's table still had a nasty sag in the middle.

Worse still, it was *very* wobbly.

Paddington decided he had an emergency on his paws.

First he sawed a piece of wood off
the longest leg . . .

. . . but that made the table wobble in the other direction.

So he tried sawing the end off one of
the other legs . . .

. . . but that only made matters worse.

Paddington lost count of the number of pieces he sawed off the legs, and it wasn't until he stood up again that he had yet another shock.

Mr. Curry's table seemed to have shrunk. In fact, he couldn't remember ever having seen such a short table before.

The article in Mrs. Brown's magazine was headed "Delight Your Family and Surprise Your Friends".

Paddington was quite sure Mr. Curry would be surprised when he saw what was left of his table, but as for delighting the Browns with a magazine rack . . . that seemed very far away.

It was much, much later that morning when he finally got back to the Browns' house, but when she saw what he'd made them, Mrs. Bird was more than delighted.

"Most useful," she said. "Now perhaps the room won't get so untidy."

"And how kind of you to make two," added Mrs. Brown.

"Er . . . well . . ." said Paddington. "I'm afraid they're not *both* for you. One's really for Mr. Curry, but I think I'll leave it on his doorstep after dark."

"After dark?" repeated Judy. "Whatever for?"

"I think I can guess," said Jonathan. "Look!"

Everybody hurried to the window in order to see what was going on outside.

"Bear!" roared Mr. Curry. "Where are you, bear?"

"Well, Paddington," said Mrs. Bird. "What have you got to say?"

"Perhaps," said Paddington hopefully, "Mr. Curry will feel better if I make him a present of my tools as well as the magazine rack.

"After to-day I don't think I shall be 'doing it myself' again for a long time!"

*This story comes from PADDINGTON HELPS OUT
and is based on the television film. It has been
specially written by Michael Bond for
younger children.*

ISBN 0 00 123209 6 (paperback)
ISBN 0 00 123216 9 (cased)
Text copyright © 1977 Michael Bond
Illustrations copyright © 1977 William Collins Sons & Co. Ltd.
Cover copyright © 1977 William Collins Sons & Co. Ltd. and Film Fair Lt
Cover design by Ivor Wood. Cover photographed by Bruce Scott.
Printed in Great Britain